WILLIAM SHAKESPEARE'S
HAMLET

Retold by BRUCE COVILLE

Pictures by LEONID GORE

Dial Books | *New York*

Published by Dial Books
A member of Penguin Group (USA) Inc.
345 Hudson Street • New York, New York 10014

Text copyright © 2004 by Bruce Coville
Pictures copyright © 2004 by Leonid Gore
All rights reserved
Designed by Atha Tehon
Text set in Bembo
Manufactured in China on acid-free paper
1 3 5 7 9 10 8 6 4 2

Library of Congress Cataloging-in-Publication Data
Coville, Bruce.
William Shakespeare's Hamlet / retold by Bruce Coville;
pictures by Leonid Gore.
p.   cm.
Summary: Retells, in simplified prose, William Shakespeare's play
about a prince of Denmark who seeks revenge for his father's murder.
ISBN 0-8037-2708-9
1. Hamlet (Legendary character)—Juvenile fiction.
2. Revenge—Juvenile fiction. 3. Denmark—Juvenile fiction.
4. Princes—Juvenile fiction.
[1. Shakespeare, William, 1564–1616—Adaptations.]
I. Shakespeare, William, 1564–1616. Hamlet.
II. Gore, Leonid, ill. III. Title.
PR2878.H3 C68 2004   822.3'3—dc21   2002013743

The paintings were done in acrylic and pastel on paper.

For Daniel Bostick—Great Actor, Great Friend
B.C.

To Atha Tehon, for sharing the doubts
L.G.